Maple & Willow
Together

Lori Nichols

Nancy Paulsen Books ✸ An Imprint of Penguin Group (USA)

For Nikki
(Orfay Imay Istersay Ikkinay)

and for my heart-rock-sister-friend Dariana

Lori would like to thank her posse of posers: H.Z.B., PK, Suzzanna, Carmine and Maddie.
Also, a belated *Maple* thanks to the entire Renneker family for their willingness to pose at the drop of a hat.
And to Fred for all his tree knowledge.

NANCY PAULSEN BOOKS
Published by the Penguin Group
Penguin Group (USA) LLC
375 Hudson Street, New York, NY 10014

USA | Canada | UK | Ireland | Australia
New Zealand | India | South Africa | China
penguin.com
A Penguin Random House Company

Library of Congress Cataloging-in-Publication Data
Nichols, Lori, author, illustrator.
Maple and Willow together / Lori Nichols.
pages cm
Summary: Nature-loving sisters Maple and Willow smooth over a rough patch in their friendship in their own unique way.
[1. Sisters—Fiction. 2. Friendship—Fiction. 3. Nature—Fiction.] I. Title.   PZ7.N5413Mc 2014   [E]—dc23   2013043045

Manufactured in China by South China Printing Co. Ltd.
ISBN 978-0-399-16283-1
1 3 5 7 9 10 8 6 4 2

Design by Marikka Tamura. Text set in LTC Kennerley Pro.
The illustrations for this book were rendered in pencil on Mylar and then digitally colored.

Maple and her little sister, Willow, were always together.

It was hard to remember a time
when the girls weren't together.

In fact, their parents
even wondered if the girls
had their own language.
And in a way, they did.

They spent mornings together . . .

and most nights.

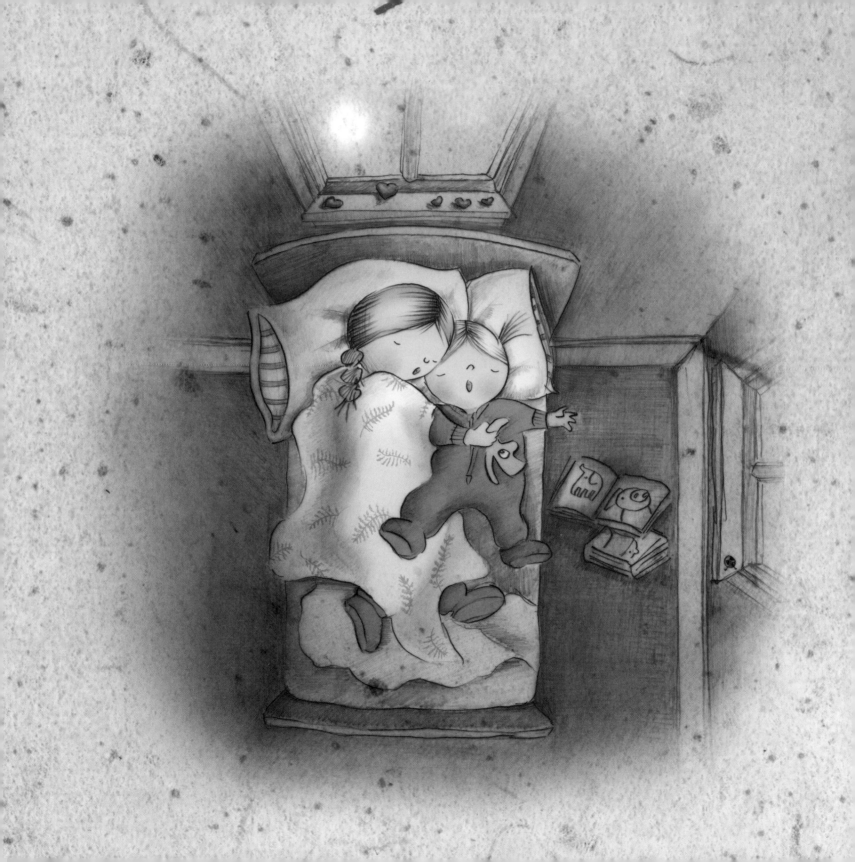

On sunny days, the girls
looked for heart rocks . . .

built fairy houses . . .
and caught grasshoppers.

Hide-and-seek was one of
their favorite games.
"You're it," Maple would shout.

−124 5 6 7 89

But Maple didn't like
the way Willow counted.

When it rained, Maple would chirp,
"I'm in charge of the umbrella!"

Willow didn't mind.
Because she was in charge of the puddles!

The puddles brought out worms.
Maple and Willow both loved worms.
Maple kept her worm in a special box.
Her box.

That was okay with Willow
because she liked her worm
to wriggle all over her fingers.

One day, Maple decided
they should pick dandelions.

Willow wanted to blow them to the wind.

But Maple wanted to
collect the dandelions—
not blow them.

That's when Willow
decided to show Maple
a thing or two.

And Maple
decided to tell Willow
a thing or two.

Then Willow took it out
on Maple's toy.

And Maple took it out on Willow.

Neither sister wanted to be together ever again.

The girls were
separated and sent
to their own rooms.

But after a while,
that got boring.

So Maple
slipped something
over to Willow.

Then Willow
slipped something
over to Maple.

The girls met halfway
and were together once again.

They couldn't wait to run back outside . . .

and this time, when
Maple and Willow
collected dandelions,

they both made wishes and
blew them to the wind.

That evening, they took a bath . . .

and put on their pajamas . . .

and hopped like grasshoppers . . .

and read more books . . .

and fell asleep,
  together.

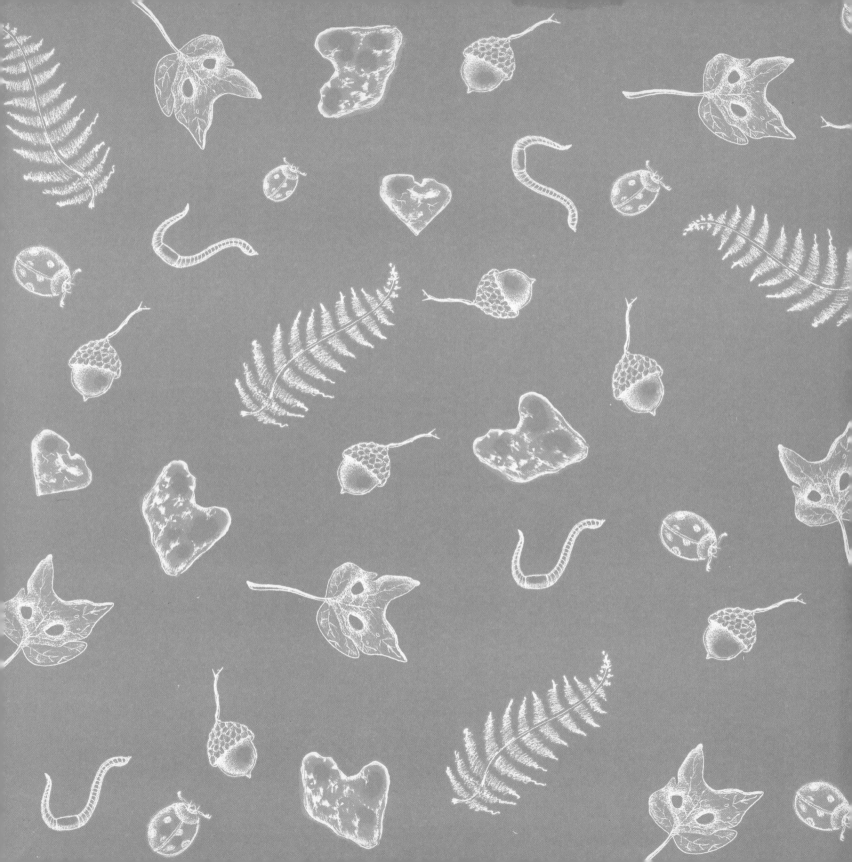